JIM ARNOSKY

Raccoon
on His Own

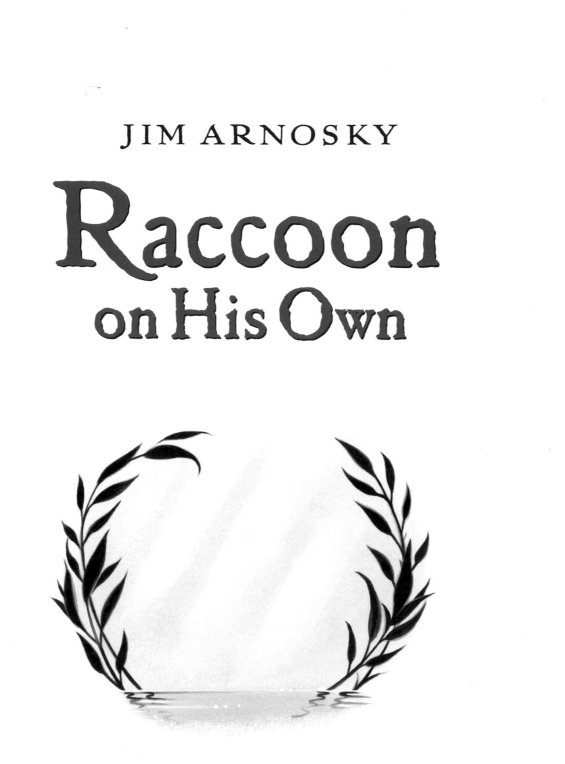

G. P. PUTNAM'S SONS / NEW YORK

Printed in Hong Kong by South China Printing Co. (1988) Ltd.
Designed by Gunta Alexander. Text set in Minister. The art was done in watercolor.

Library of Congress Cataloging-in-Publication Data
Arnosky, Jim. Raccoon on his own / Jim Arnosky.   p.   cm.   Summary: A curious young raccoon
takes an unexpected trip downstream in a small wooden boat. 1. Raccoons—Juvenile fiction.
[1. Raccoons—Fiction.] I. Title. PZ10.3.A.86923 Do 2001 [E]—dc21 00-059160
ISBN 0-399-22756-3   10 9 8 7 6 5 4 3 2 1   First Impression

For Hailey

In the dark swamp, a new day dawned
like a sleepy eye, opening slowly.
A small wooden boat floated,
nudged against some mud.

The mud was soft and sandy.
A mother raccoon with her young
came to dig and search for food.

Mother found a crunchy crawfish.
Two of the young raccoons dug
for crawfish near the boat.
The third young raccoon
was not hungry.
He wanted
to climb.

The hungry raccoons
quickly dug up all the mud
around the boat.
With no sticky mud to hold it,
the boat began to float away.

The raccoon in the boat looked up.

A chill ran down his spine.

He was drifting in the boat, alone.

He was on his own for the very first time.

Afraid to jump into the dark water,

he stared back at the mud bank.

The boat silently carried him downstream.

The raccoon reached up
to grab a sturdy branch
and climb out of the moving boat.
But the branch was too high.

The boat glided
under another branch.
This branch was low enough to climb.
But the raccoon saw the shape of a long snake
draped across the branch, and he ducked down.

He crawled to the other end of the boat.
Downstream, he saw shadowy shapes
of plants and trees
sticking up out of the water.
The raccoon looked down
into the dark stream
and saw a raccoon looking back!
His reflection kept him company
as the boat moved along,
through air so still,
on water so smooth.

As the boat passed through
a bunch of water lilies,
something huge made a great splash.

It was a great big alligator
that had been hiding
under the lily pads.

"Zweet, zweet, zweet,"
came a sound from above.
The raccoon looked up
and saw five young warblers.
"Zweet, zweet, zweet,"
the birds called down.
The raccoon "churred" back.

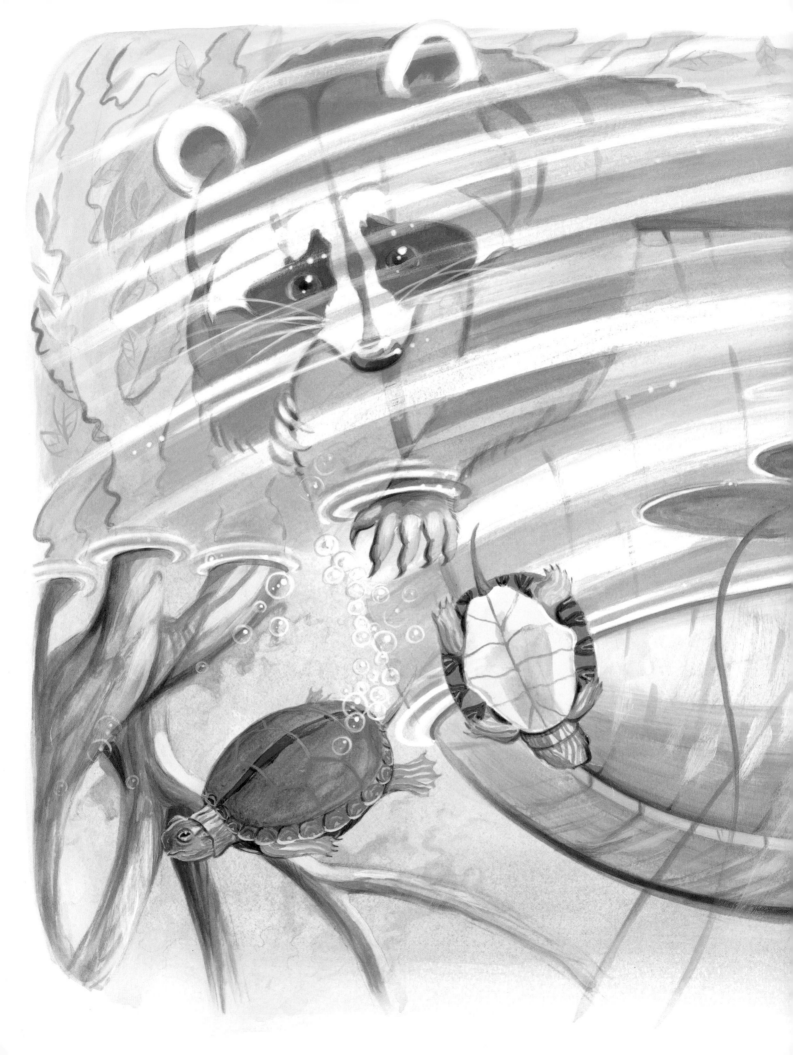

Three tiny turtles swam up to the boat.
The raccoon reached into the water
to touch one turtle's shell,
and all three scattered away.

A mother merganser paddled by,
leading her nine little ducklings.
The raccoon watched the ducklings
swimming close to their mother.

Suddenly, the boat bumped
into another mud bank
and stopped.
The raccoon saw his family
coming to meet him.
He ran to his mother.

And just like that,
they were all together again.
Downstream.